JUST KISS ME

憋说话，吻我

［俄］兰迪诗 / 著绘
董乐乐 / 译

時代文藝出版社

图书在版编目（CIP）数据

憋说话，吻我 /（俄罗斯）兰迪诗著绘；董乐乐译.
— 长春：时代文艺出版社，2016.3
ISBN 978-7-5387-5151-2
Ⅰ.①憋… Ⅱ.①兰… ②董… Ⅲ.①漫画－作品集－俄罗斯－现代
Ⅳ.①J238.2

中国版本图书馆CIP数据核字(2016)第007108号

出品人 陈 琛
产品总监 郭力家
责任编辑 曾艳纯
助理编辑 冯 卓
项目策划 紫图图书ZITO®
监 制 黄 利 万 夏
丛书主编 郎世溟
特约编辑 宣佳丽 刘长娥 朱彦沛
装帧设计 紫图图书ZITO®

憋说话，吻我

[俄] 兰迪诗/著绘 董乐乐/译

出版发行 / 时代文艺出版社
地址 / 长春市泰来街1825号 时代文艺出版社 邮编 / 130011
总编办 / 0431－86012927 发行部 / 0431－86012957 北京开发部 / 010－63108163
网址 / www.shidaicn.com
印刷 / 北京中科印刷有限公司
开本 / 720毫米×1000毫米 1 / 16 字数 / 80千字 印张 /11
版次 / 2016年3月第1版 印次 / 2016年7月第3次印刷 定价 / 42.00元

图书如有印装错误 请寄回印厂调换

CONTENTS 目录

献给所有追爱的人

MY LOVER LIVES IN THE FUTURE

我只不过在谈一场异地恋，
他住在未来

大家总说，你的真命天子早晚都会来，

我在想，我的真命天子是不是在来的路上被车撞了。

No, I am not single.
I am in a long distance
relationship because
my girlfriend lives in the

FUTURE

我不是单身狗，

我只不过是在谈一场异地恋，

我的女朋友住在未来。

I'm worried that I may have already met the man of my dreams, but I probably told him to fuck off.

我担心我已经见过我的梦中情人了，

但我好像叫他滚了。

Dear future husband,
I hope you're a good cook.

亲爱的未来老公，
希望你会做饭。

The brain is the most
outstanding organ.
It works 24 hours a day
365 days a year from
birth until you fall in love.

大脑是人体中最出色的器官。
从你出生的那天开始，它每天要工作 24 小时，
全年 365 天无休，
直到你爱上某个人。

Guys I find attractive:

—Famous

—Taken

—Twice my age

—Don't know I exist

—Not real

我喜欢的男生：

——明星

——名草有主

——年纪是我的两倍

——不知道我存在

——不是现实中的人

我男朋友就像 -1 的平方根——虚构的。

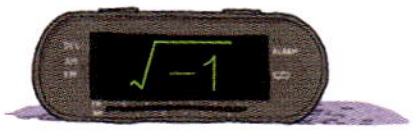

Will you date me?
Breathe if yes,
recite the Bible in Japanese if no.

你同意跟我约会吗？
同意的话就呼吸，
不同意就用日语背一遍圣经。

I'm single by choice.
Not my choice, but still a choice.

我单身是选择的结果。
不是我选择了单身，而是单身选择了我。

Dear me ,
you're the sexiest thing
that has ever
walked this earth!
Love, me!

亲爱的我，
你是地球上曾有过的最性感的人！
爱我！

Relationship status:

☐ Single
☐ In a relationship
☐ Married
☐ Engaged
☐ Divorced
☑ Waiting for a miracle

感情状况：

☐ 单身
☐ 恋爱中
☐ 已婚
☐ 订婚
☐ 离婚
☑ 在等一个奇迹

Why I'm single:

- [x] I can't date the internet.
- [x] I can't date my favorite celebrity.
- [x] I can't date myself.
- [x] I can't date music.

我单身的原因：

- [x] 我不能跟网络谈恋爱。
- [x] 我不能跟我最喜欢的明星谈恋爱。
- [x] 我不能跟自己谈恋爱。
- [x] 我不能跟音乐谈恋爱。

Stalking is when two people go
for a long romantic walk together,
but only one of them knows about it.

跟踪是指
两个人浪漫地同行了很长时间，
但是只有一个人知道。

Grow a beard and then we'll talk.

等你长大了我们再谈恋爱吧。

当你看到一个超正的帅哥的时候，

你都想握住他妈妈的手，

真挚地说一句“干得好”。

Note to self:
Try your best.
Not to stare at him.
(It's creepy!)

提醒自己：
努力。
不要总盯着他看。
（太令人毛骨悚然了！）

Someone cute walks past

Me:"noooo, come back.

I love you..."

当可爱的姑娘从我身边走过时

“别走！你回来！

我喜欢你……”

When people ask:
"How are you still single? You are good looking, nice and you always listen..."
My reply is: "I'm overqualified."

每当有人对我说：
“你怎么还单身呢？你长得不赖，人也挺好，善于倾听……”
我就会说：“我的条件太好了，所以才找不到对象。”

Just because I don't have a boyfriend,
it doesn't mean I'm alone.
I have food and the internet.

我没有男朋友
不代表我单身。
我有好吃的，还有网络。

I want to be the reason
you look down at
your phone and smile.
Then walk into a pole.

真希望我是那个让你盯着手机傻笑，

……

傻到走路撞上电线杆子的人。

当我的意中人只给我回复了
一个"K"(OK的意思)的时候,
我心里想的是,"Kiss是以K开头的"。

——你跟女孩子约会过吗？

——应该说成功了一半。

——什么意思？

——我去了，但她没去。

我从来不觉得自己能追上谁。

把人追得抓狂也挺好的。

如何才能找到男朋友：

1. 我也不知道。

2. 哭去吧。

I hope one day I will love
something the way women
in commercial love
yoghurt.

我希望有一天自己能无可救药地爱上一个人，

就像广告里，女人无可救药地爱上了一盒酸奶那样。

注：love something 直译“爱上某个事物”，此处译为“爱上一个人”是为了配合全书主题而译。

JUST KISS ME

憋说话，吻我

I like when you smile.
But I love it
when I am the reason.

我喜欢看你笑。
那笑容若是因我，
我便更喜欢了。

Are you a dementor?
Cos you take my breath away!

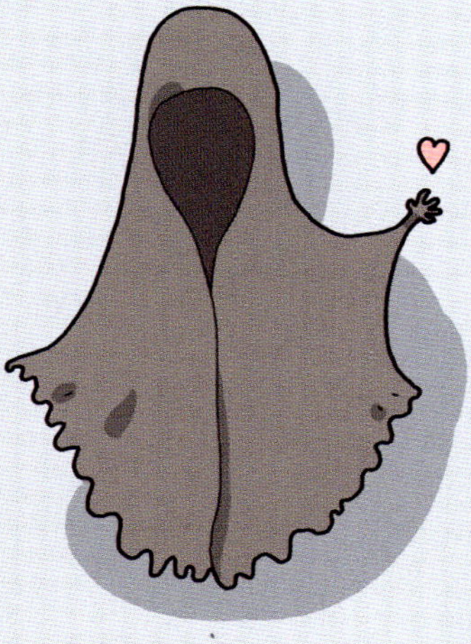

你是摄魂怪吗？你让我无法呼吸。

I don't know what
I would do without you,
but I bet it would be awesome.

我不知道没有你自己会怎样，
但我想一定很糟糕。

让我看看你的手机。

删除……
删除……
删除……
删除……
删除……
删除……

给你。

如何让女人发狂？只需要两个步骤：

1. 给她拍张照片。

2. 不给她看。

一定要是和我一样的怪人！

一定要是和我一样的怪人！

一定要是和我一样的怪人！

——每次和人约会时，我都会默默祈祷。

I hate mosquitoes just like everyone, but I love the fact that their presence allows me to slap anyone, at any time, for no reason at all.

我跟所有人一样讨厌蚊子，但是有蚊子时，

我可以随时随地扇人巴掌，不用费尽心思想理由，

这一点倒是挺好的。

She asked me to hug her for warmth…
But, evil genius as I am,
I hugged her to warm myself.

她说冷，要抱抱……
我心里奸笑着想到，你以为占便宜的是你，
其实是我，我抱你我自己也暖和。

You're the best *
thing in my life.

BESIDES COFFEE.

你是我生命中最美好的存在，

咖啡也是。

I love you because

we hate the same stuff.

我爱你，是因为

我们讨厌相同的东西。

If you're too busy
to chat with me,
I'd better not see you online!

如果你太忙不能跟我聊天，
最好别让我看见你在线！

We always hold hands.
If I let go, she shops.
—Henry Youngman

我们俩总是手拉着手，
因为我一放手，她就去买买买。
——亨利·杨格曼

All you need is love.
But a little chocolate
now and then doesn't hurt.

你需要的只是爱。
但是，不时来块巧克力也没什么不好。

找一天去吃个晚饭吧？

哦，我天天都得吃晚饭啊。

言语无法表达

你对我有多重要。

注：送 espresso（意式咖啡）给喜欢的人，表示：“words cannot express how much you mean to me.”图片英文中“espresso”是双关用法。

You text him, he doesn't text back. He was obviously so excited that you texted him that he fainted.

你给他发短信，他没回。

他肯定是因为接到你的短信太兴奋，昏倒了。

和我约会的两点理由：

1. 没有人能把我从你身边抢走。

2. 有时候我也挺有趣的。

如果有Wi-Fi，
谁还有工夫吵架？

If you're wrong and you shut up,
you're wise.
If you're right and you shut up,
you're married.

如果你做错事不狡辩，
说明你是个聪明人。
如果你做对了也不争辩，
说明你已经结婚了。

My wife is weird. She starts every conversation with: "Were you even listening to me?"

我老婆特怪。
她每次说话都会先说上一句：
“你刚才在听我说话吗？”

I haven't talked to my wife for three weeks. I didn't want to interrupt her.

我已经三周没跟我老婆说过话了。

我不想打断她。

A man's house is his castle
until the queen comes home.

对于一个男人来说，他的房子就是他的城堡，
但是等到房子有了女主人，就不是那么回事儿了。

——“我想邀你出去。”

——“邀我出去？你就不想让我在舒心的地方待着吗？”

当我喜欢上一个人的时候：

1%——告白；

99%——盯着人家傻看。

Kiss me!

吻我！

English Game:
Place the word "only"
anywhere in the sentence:
She told him that she loved him.

造句游戏：
把"只"这个字放到下面的句子里：
她对他说她爱他。

别人是怎么追女神的呢？

我连在麦当劳多要一点番茄酱的勇气都没有。

They told me that
to make her fall in love,
I had to make her laugh.
But every time she laughs
I'm the one who falls in love.

他们说要让她心动的话，我就逗她笑。

但是，她每次一笑，我就会更爱她。

如果你喜欢水，

说明你已经喜欢上 72% 的我了！

SINGLE
我只是和别人不一样

Everything I like is either
expensive, fattening or
won't text me.

我喜欢的东西，
不是太贵，就是会让人发胖，
要不就是不回我短信。

我找男朋友比莱昂纳多·迪卡普里奥得奥斯卡还难。

我最喜欢的户外运动就是回到室内。

A computer once beat me at chess,
but it was no match for me
at kick-boxing.

下棋的时候，电脑让我输得一败涂地。
但是自由搏击，它肯定不是我的对手。

你可以对自己提出问题，
也可以自己找到答案，
只有当你觉得自己做错了，
才会想要原谅自己。

I wonder,

we lazy people go to heaven

or they send someone

to pick us up?

我在想，

我们这些懒人是怎么上天堂的，

他们是不是还得派人来接我们呀？

When inspiration
does not come to me,
I go halfway to meet it.
—Sigmund Freud

每当灵感不来找我，我就去半路跟它会合。

——西格蒙德·弗洛伊德

不能说我字写得丑，

我只是用了自己独创的字体而已。

I need an undo button
for my mouth.

真想给我的嘴巴装上一个撤销按钮。

I have a disease called awesome.
You won't understand it
since you don't have it.

我得了一种名为“酷毙了”的病。
你不会懂，
毕竟你没得这种病。

At the gym I'm like ninja.
You will never see me there.

在健身房，我就像忍者一样。
你永远找不到我的身影。

A queen is never late.

Everyone else is simply early.

女王从不会迟到，

只是其他人早到了而已。

我没有生气。我很淡定。

I'm planning on avoiding
embarrassing tan lines
by strictly sticking
to indoor activities.

为了避免晒黑，

我决定只在房间里活动。

我才不在乎你怎么看我，

除非你觉得我特帅。

毕竟你说对了。

With the right music
you can forget anything,
or remember everything.

好音乐能让你忘掉任何事，
也可能会让所有往事涌上心头。

飞行我是不怕的，

我怕的是飞着飞着突然不飞了。

I hate when I'm about to hug someone really sexy and my face hits mirror.

真是恨哪！

当我看见一个超级性感的人，

要和他拥抱时，脸却碰到了镜子。

Never get into
an argument
with someone
who types faster
than you.

永远不要跟打字比你快的人吵架。

I'd rather enter
a coma than a gym.

我宁愿昏过去也不想动起来。

生命短暂，时间宝贵，

怎么能把宝贵的时间浪费在

安全移除移动硬盘这种小事上！

在没有这几位猫主子之前，

我是个正常人。

注：three cats ago，把猫借用为时间单位，意指主人公养过几只猫之前。

我就跟iPhone一样，
什么都不干也会耗电。

That awkward moment
when you get home and
look at yourself in the
mirror thinking...
Did I really look like this all day?

当你回到家，看着镜子里的自己想……

我今天一天都是这副德行吗？

这个时刻实在是太尴尬了。

If you always do what interests you,
at least one person is pleased.
—Katharine Hepburn

如果你一直做自己感兴趣的事，
至少自己是开心的。
——凯瑟琳·赫本

Dance like no one is watching.
Because everyone is on their phone,
so no one is watching.

别不好意思，

就当只有自己一个人，尽情跳舞吧。

反正其他人都在看手机，没人看你的。

人家不是懒惰，

人家是猫系女。

Smiling gives you wrinkles,
resting bitch face
keeps you pretty.

笑容会让你满脸皱纹，
臭脸才会让你永葆靓丽。

情感状况：吃。

There's always one of
those days where
your middle finger is
an answer to every question.

总是有那么几天，
想用中指回答所有的问题。

我是那种会从健身房里走出来的人，严格来讲，

我是那种会从健身房走出来……直奔麦当劳的人。

This will be us when we're old...

(I can't wait.)

P.S. I hope your boobs sag first.

这就是我们老了以后的样子……

（有点迫不及待）

P.S. 我希望你的咪咪先下垂。

programmer

n. [proh-gram-er]

an organism that turns caffeine
and pizza into software.

程序员是一种神奇的动物，

喝进去的是咖啡，吃进去的是披萨，

挤出来的是代码。

I got covered in ketchup earlier today, from my head tomatoes.

今天早晨我把番茄酱洒了一身，

没想到我就这么红了。

注："I love ketchup from my head tomatoes." 是一句世界流行语。"tomatoes" 是 "to my toes" 的谐音，常用在海报、文化衫和贺卡上。

——你把巧克力酱藏在哪了？

——我不告诉你。

注：nutelling 意指不告诉、不说，常用英文应为”not telling“。这里是为了保持英文的趣味性，与“nutella”中部分成分“nutell”一致。

I HAVE A DREAM

我有一个梦想

我一年只想放两次假，
每次放六个月就够了。

Sometimes when I say "I'm okay",
what I really want is
for someone to hold my hand,
look me in the eyes and say:
"You're not okay, here is $1000."

当我说"我没事"的时候，
其实是希望有个人能拉着我的手，深情地望着我说：
"我知道你有事，这是1000块钱，拿去吧。"

Too easy to achieve,
is not called dream.

太容易实现的，
那就不叫梦想。

For my birthday give me money,
it goes with anything.

我过生日的时候真的不用送我礼物，
直接给钱就行了，我自己会买。

我对未来的规划，
从“等我有钱了”开始。

I love days when
my only problem is

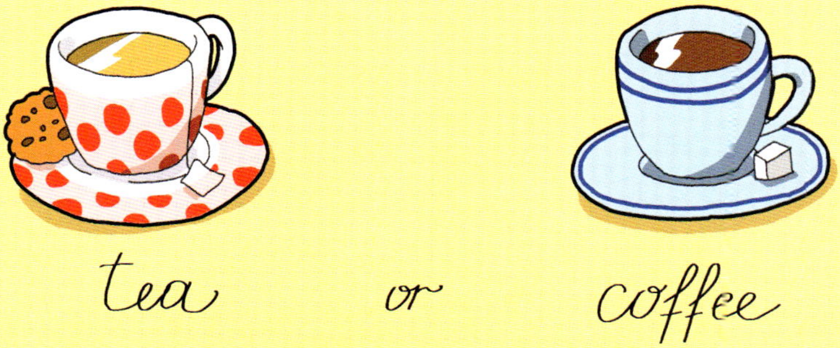

我热爱生活，

如果我面临的难题只是要喝

茶还是咖啡。

Food for thought

will eat anything edible.

精神食粮

能吃的都不放过。

Some days I just wish I could be transformed into a little penguin. That way I could completely ignore all of my human responsibilities.

有时候，我真希望自己变成一只小企鹅。

这样一来，我就不用肩负生而为人的责任了。

I like cooking my family
and my pets.
Use commas.
Don't be a psycho.

我喜欢烹饪我的家人和我的宠物。
加上逗号，
不然别人会以为你疯了。

注：我喜欢烹饪，我的家人和我的宠物。

Harry Potter fans:

I wanna go to Hogwarts.

Narnia fans:

I wanna go to Narnia.

Hunger Games fans:

Nope, I'm good.

《哈利·波特》粉：

我想去霍格沃茨。

《纳尼亚传奇》粉：

我想去纳尼亚。

《饥饿游戏》粉：

我哪也不想去，这儿挺好。

Pros and cons of making food

Pros: food

Cons: making

给做饭投反对票或赞成票

赞成：饭

反对：做

I was supposed to have
a nice body for people
to look at this summer.

But there is one small problem…
I love food more
than I love people.

我希望今年夏天能给大家展现一副好身材，

但是有个小问题……

我在乎大家的看法，但我更在乎好吃的。

根据天文学，你对着流星许愿时，一切都已经晚了，

那颗流星是在数百万年前划过那片天空的。

那颗流星早已不复存在。

就像你的梦想一样。

I want to write a mystery novel… or do I?

—Stewart Francis

我想写一部推理小说……

写还是不写呢？真相只有一个。

——斯图尔特·弗兰西斯

Basic human needs

人类基本需求

自我实现的需求

尊重的需求

情感和归属的需求

安全上的需求

生理上的需求

Wi-Fi

Procrastination? No. I just wait until the last second to do my work. Because I will be older, therefore wiser.

拖延？不是那么回事，

我只是等到最后期限再做。

因为那时候我又年长了一点，变得更加智慧了。

Knowledge is power,
and power corrupts.
So study hard and be evil.

知识就是力量，
力量滋生腐败。
所以努力学习，当个大魔王吧。

The ugly people
should read more books.
Because knowledge
can change the fate.

人丑就该多读书，
因为知识改变命运。

Your future depends
on your dreams,
so go to sleep.

梦想决定未来。
所以，赶紧去睡吧。

Women who seek to be equal
with men lack ambition.

—Marilyn Monroe

只有没有野心的女人才会追求男女平等。

——玛丽莲·梦露

明天——一个神秘的地方，

在那里，99%的人勤劳积极，

人们在那个地方获得了无数成就。

BORN TO EAT

不是肚子饿，只是嘴巴太寂寞

Everybody has a girlfriend or a boyfriend.
And I'm just over here like
"I love food".

没有女朋友的，都有男朋友了。
此时此刻的我也有爱慕的对象，我想说：
"我爱吃！"

I want to have a nice body, but
not as much as I want dessert.

瘦，我所欲也；
甜点，亦我所欲也；
二者不可得兼，
舍瘦而取甜点者也。

啤酒是好东西。

有比啤酒更好的吗？

有，那就是一大堆啤酒。

I don't fight my way
to the top of the food chain
to be a vegetarian.

我费了那么大劲儿
爬到食物链顶端
不是为了吃素的。

If pigs really could fly,
I bet their wings would
taste absolutely delicious.

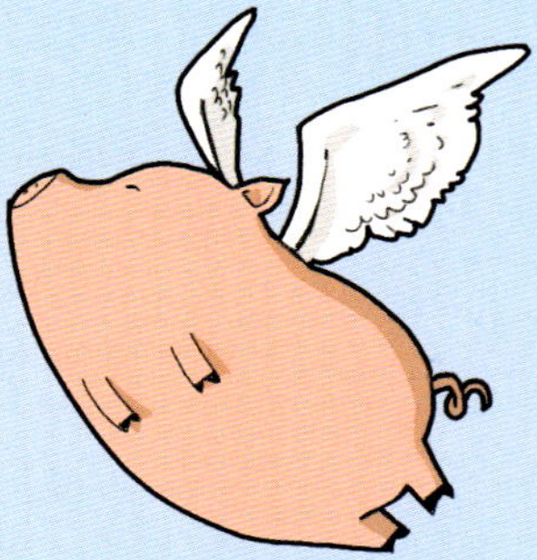

如果猪真的会飞，

我敢打赌

猪翅一定很好吃……

The biggest part of my day I spend
just keeping myself distracted until
it's time to eat food again.

大部分时间我都处在失魂落魄的状态，

只有一件事能让我专心致志：

又到吃饭的时间啦～

I have a condition that
makes me eat when I can't sleep.
It's called
insom-nom-nom-nom-nom-nia.

我得了一种病，
睡不着觉的时候就得吃东西，
这种病叫失眠吧唧-吧唧-吧唧症。

—If you have 10 cookies and someone takes half of them, what will they have?

—A broken hand.

——如果你有十块饼干，有人拿走了一半，

那个人得到了多少？

——一……只被我打伤的手。

You can't buy happiness
but you can buy ice-cream.
And that's kind of the same thing.

钱买不到幸福，
但是钱可以买到冰激凌。
吃上冰激凌谁还会觉得不幸福？

There's a skinny girl who lives inside of me that's trying to get out but I usually can shut her up with cookies.

其实我身体里住着一个瘦子，

但是我一直往嘴里塞饼干，

挡住了她唯一的出路。

A balanced diet means
a cupcake in each hand.

所谓的平衡饮食是指
左手拿起一块蛋糕，右手也不能空着。

Accidentally went grocery shopping
on an empty stomach and now
I'm the proud owner of aisle 4.

一不小心空着肚子逛超市去了，

这下好了，5排货架上的东西全是我的了。

在食物这个问题上，

没有“我们”，都是“我”的。

My favorite ice cream
flavour is more.

我最喜欢的冰激凌是：大桶的。

我最爱的运动就是：吃。

A yawn is
a silent scream
for coffee.

打哈欠是对咖啡无声的召唤。

如果没人看见你吃东西，

你就可以当作没吃。

——弗兰，那是两个。

——不，这样吃，身体不会知道。

不是肚子饿，只是嘴巴太寂寞。

It may look like I'm having
really deep thoughts, but
99% of the time I'm just thinking
about what food I'm going
to eat later.

在别人眼里，我是个思考者。
他们没看错，只是我99%的时间都在思考，
一会儿吃什么。

Eat anything you want,
and if people make fun of
your weight, eat them too.

想吃什么就吃什么，
如果有人嘲笑你胖，没关系，
把他也吃了。

Fri**end**

Best fri**end**

Boyfri**end**

Girlfri**end**

Food

Only food has no **end**…

朋友、好朋友、男朋友、女朋友，都有个end，

能不离不弃的只有食物……

I love my six pack so much
I protect it with a layer of fat.

我超爱我的六块腹肌，

为了保护它们，

我特意在上面盖上了一层肥肉。

In the morning I can't eat, I'm thinking of you.

In the evening I can't eat, I'm thinking of you.

In the night I can't sleep...

I'm so hungry!

早晨，我吃不下饭，因为我想你。

晚上，我吃不下饭，因为我想你。

半夜，我睡不着觉……

因为我饿了！

I'm still trying to
get over the fact
that oranges are
pre-sliced
by nature.

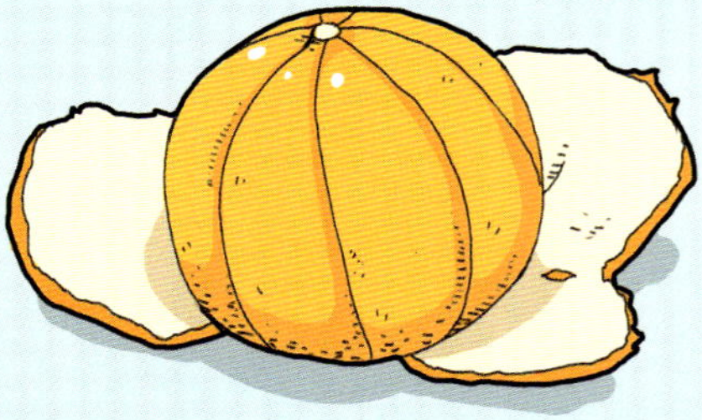

我一直在琢磨一个事：

桔子竟然是一种天生就切好了的水果。

I keep losing weight,
but it keeps finding me.

我一直在甩肉，
但是肉一直在粘我。

大腿没有腿缝的额外福利：

好吃的掉到腿上的时候，你能接住。

I eat cake because
it's somebody's
birthday
somewhere.

我之所以吃蛋糕是因为
世界那么大，肯定有人今天过生日。

I would lose weight
but I hate losing...

我想减肥，但我讨厌失去……

If your thighs touch you're
one step closer to being a mermaid,
so who's the real winner here?

如果你的两条大腿挨得太近，
说明你离美人鱼又近了一步。
所以，你觉得谁更美？

吃而无憾!

Don't be afraid of
a few extra pounds.
Fat people are harder
to kidnap.

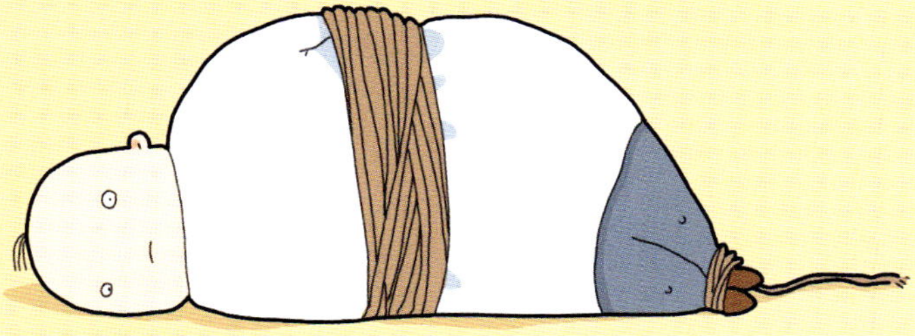

胖了几斤真不是什么大不了的事儿。

如果有人想绑架你，

他都得算计算计绳子的成本。

到该吃蛋糕的时间啦。

If a 99-pound girl
eats 1 pound of nachos,
she is 1% nacho.

如果一个99磅的女生吃了1磅的玉米片，
那她就不是100%的女生了，因为她有1%是玉米片。

生命诚可贵，油炸食品不可抛！

注：改编自俗语 get rich or die tryin 要钱不要命，直译为“要油炸食品不要命”。

I WANT TO MARRY MY BED

都别拦我，我只想嫁给我的床

我也不是不能早起，

只要改改早晨的定义就成，

比如说把早晨的时间改成12点前后。

Man, time really flies,
when you take two naps a day.

哥们儿，当你一天睡两次觉时，
时间就过得飞快。

I have decide to take
exercise more seriously.
Today I move to the left.
Tomorrow I go right.

我已经决定了，运动这事不能再光说不练了。

今天我向左翻，明天向右翻。

Am I the only one who calculates
how much sleep I can get
before going to bed?

在上床睡觉之前，
我会计算一下这一觉能睡多长时间。
只有我一个人会这样做吗？

一首关于起床的小诗：
不起，不起，不起，
就不起；
不起，不起，不起，
说什么我都不起……

Damn right I'm good in bed.
I can stay there all day.

在床上的感觉太好了，
我可以待上一整天。

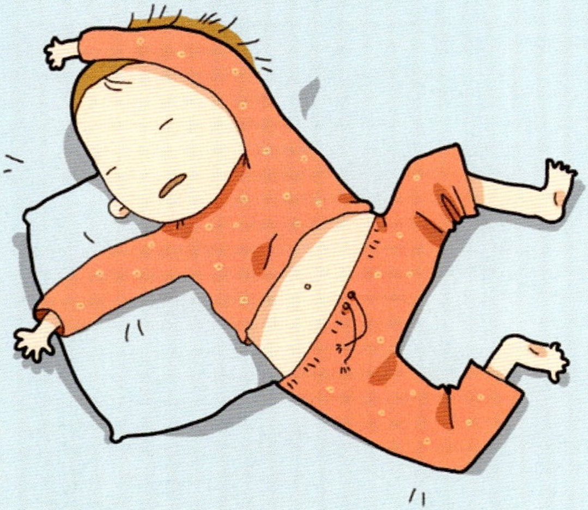

Clinomania

(n.) excessive desire to stay in bed.

恋床癖

过度渴望待在床上。

Today will be one of those
days that even my coffee
will need a coffee.

今天属于那种
就连我的咖啡
都想来杯咖啡提提神的日子。

我并不是只喜欢在家闷头睡大觉，

我也喜欢聚会，

反正聚会对我来说就是换个地方打盹儿。

Asked my heart why
I can't sleep at night.
My heart replied ,
"Because you slept in the afternoon.
Don't act like you're in love."

我扪心自问："为什么晚上睡不着觉呢？"
我的心脏回答我说："因为你下午已经睡过一大觉了，
别装得恋爱了似的。"

I think when you dream at night,
your eyes turn all the way around,
so you can see what's inside your head.

当你做梦的时候，

你的眼睛一直在转，

所以你能看到你脑子里想的是什么。

Do you ever just
wake up and go?
"Nope."
...And roll over and
go back to sleep?

你有没有醒了以后就起来?
"没有。"
……然后翻个身接着睡觉?

明明起床的时候像个丑鬼，

怎么还叫“睡美容觉”呢？

注：troll 是北欧神话（即斯堪的纳维亚神话）中的丑陋怪物。

Keep the dream alive:
Hit the snooze button.

有梦就要坚持：
闹钟响了就赶紧关掉。

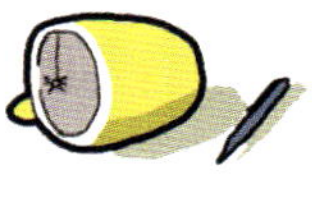

我也有不毒舌的时候，

毕竟我也得睡觉。

I have to exercise early in
the morning before my brain
figures out what I'm doing.

我必须早起做运动，
趁我脑子还没清醒过来。

Remember the sloths: they don't do
anything and haven't gone extinct.
I'm sure you can afford to take a nap.

看看树懒，它们一天到晚什么也不干，居然也没灭亡。

我觉得，有一件事你还是有能力完成的，比如打个盹。

Don't wake me up, unless the house is on fire or you have food for me. Otherwise google your problems.

别扰了我的清梦，

除非房子着火了，或者你有好吃的要给我。

有事的话别找我，找谷歌。

今天要做的事情是：

1. 起床。

2. 存活一天。

3. 上床睡觉。

Happiness is

...not having to set the
alarm for the next day.

幸福就是不用为第二天设置闹钟。

TO BE CONTINUED

未完待续